Spin

The House That Witchy Built

The House That Witchy Built

By Dianne de Las Casas

Illustrated by Holly Stone-Barker

PELICAN PUBLISHING COMPANY

GRETNA 2011

To my spooktacular team at Pelican: Nina, Caitlin,
Katie, and Scott—Dianne de Las Casas

To Stephen, no bones about it . . . you rock!
To Ella, my precious little BOO!—Holly Stone-Barker

The word "Pelican" and the depiction of a pelican are trademarks
of Pelican Publishing Company, Inc., and are registered in the
U.S. Patent and Trademark Office.

Library of Congress Cataloging-in-Publication Data

De Las Casas, Dianne.
  The house that Witchy built / by Dianne de Las Casas ; illustrated by Holly
Stone-Barker.
    p. cm.
  Summary: A scary Halloween version of "The House that Jack Built,"
featuring a witch, black cat, skeleton, and other spooky images.
  ISBN 978-1-58980-965-9 (hardcover : alk. paper) [1. Witches—Fiction. 2.
Halloween—Fiction.] I. Stone-Barker, Holly, ill. II. Title.

  PZ7.D33953Ho 2011
  [E]—dc22

                                    2011004640

Printed in Singapore
Published by Pelican Publishing Company, Inc.
1000 Burmaster Street, Gretna, Louisiana 70053

This is the **house** (creak, creak)
That Witchy built (clap, clap, clap, clap)

This is the cat (meow, meow)
That lived in the house (creak, creak)
That Witchy built (clap, clap, clap, clap)

This is the **bat** (flap, flap)
That landed on the cat (meow, meow)
That lived in the house (creak, creak)
That Witchy built (clap, clap, clap, clap)

flap, flap

boo! boo!

This is the **ghost** (boo! boo!)
That spooked the bat (flap, flap)
That landed on the cat (meow, meow)
That lived in the house (creak, creak)
That Witchy built (clap, clap, clap, clap)

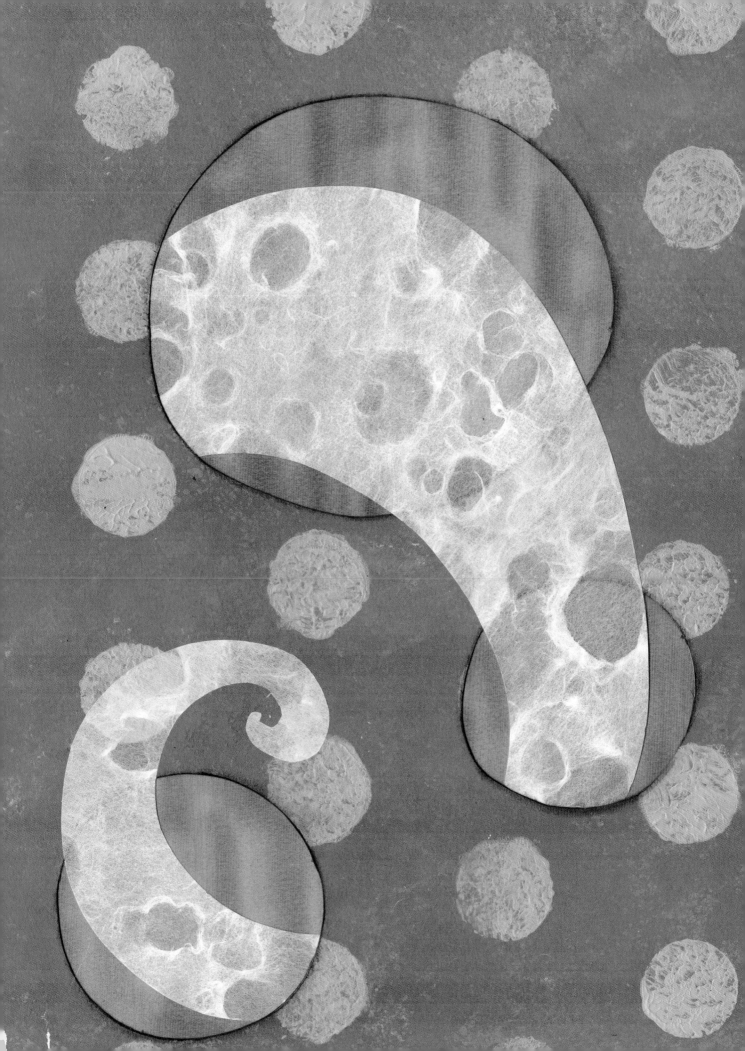

This is the **skeleton** (rattle, rattle)
That chased the ghost (boo! boo!)
That spooked the bat (flap, flap)
That landed on the cat (meow, meow)
That lived in the house (creak, creak)
That Witchy built (clap, clap, clap, clap)

yum, yum

This is the **pumpkin** (yum, yum)
That rolled after the skeleton (rattle, rattle)
That chased the ghost (boo! boo!)
That spooked the bat (flap, flap)
That landed on the cat (meow, meow)
That lived in the house (creak, creak)
That Witchy built (clap, clap, clap, clap)

RIP

Olive Yu
We love
you too!

RIP

Sandy Beeches
The Heavenly
tropics await....

creak, creak

rattle, rattle

yum, yum

RIP

Imma Star
Who lived life
with a sparkle

flap, flap

boo! boo!

meow, meow

RIP

Here lies
Rita Goodbook
On to the next
chapter

This is the **boy** (yuck, yuck)
That picked the pumpkin (yum, yum)
That rolled after the skeleton (rattle, rattle)
That chased the ghost (boo! boo!)
That spooked the bat (flap, flap)
That landed on the cat (meow, meow)
That lived in the house (creak, creak)
That Witchy built (clap, clap, clap, clap)

yuck, yuck

RIP

Here lies
Rita Goodbook
On to the next
chapter

This is the **mom** (no! no!)
That fussed at the boy (yuck, yuck)
That picked the pumpkin (yum, yum)
That rolled after the skeleton (rattle, rattle)
That chased the ghost (boo! boo!)
That spooked the bat (flap, flap)
That landed on the cat (meow, meow)
That lived in the house (creak, creak)
That Witchy built (clap, clap, clap, clap)

smooch, smooch

This is the **dad** (smooch, smooch)
That kissed the mom (no! no!))
That fussed at the boy (yuck, yuck)
That picked the pumpkin (yum, yum)
That rolled after the skeleton (rattle, rattle)
That chased the ghost (boo! boo!)
That spooked the bat (flap, flap)
That landed on the cat (meow, meow)
That lived in the house (creak, creak)
That Witchy built (clap, clap, clap, clap)

This is the
witch
(cackle, cackle)

That SPOOKED
them all
(cackle, cackle)

cackle, cackle

cackle, cackle

That flew over the dad (smooch, smooch)

RIP

Happy Cook
He found the
pie in the sky

smooch, smooch

rattle, rattle
creak, creak
yum, yum
yuck, yuck
no! no!
RIP
Olive Yu
We love you too!
RIP
Here lies
Rita Goodbook
On to the next chapter

flap, flap

That kissed the mom (no! no!))
That fussed at the boy (yuck, yuck)
That picked the pumpkin (yum, yum)
That rolled after the skeleton (rattle, rattle)
That chased the ghost (boo! boo!)
That spooked the bat (flap, flap)
That landed on the cat (meow, meow)
That lived in the house (creak, creak)
That Witchy built (clap, clap, clap, clap)

boo! boo!

meow, meow

RIP

Yuwanna
Boogy
Dancing on
Cloud 9...

Author's Note

This story is "built" on the rhythmic pattern of the old Mother Goose tale "The House That Jack Built." As a professional storyteller, I have been spinning this fun, interactive yarn for several years, and it has become a popular, highly requested story. Holly's cut-paper and collage technique never fails to astound me. She sees the extraordinary in the ordinary. Mulberry paper, wet and torn, becomes a fuzzy cat while painted wallpaper becomes skeleton bones. Amazing! I hope you enjoy this frightfully fun fable.

BOO to you!